What a Night, Charlie Brown!

Charles M. Schulz

SCHOLASTIC BOOK SERVICES

NEW YORK • TORONTO • LONDON • AUCKLAND • SYDNEY • TOKYO

Copyright © 1978 by United Feature Syndicate, Inc. Produced in association with Lee Mendelson-Bill Melendez TV Production and Charles M. Schulz Creative Associates, Warren Lockhard, President. Based upon the Lee Mendelson-Bill Melendez television production "WHAT A NIGHTMARE, CHARLIE BROWN" (© 1978 United Feature Syndicate, Inc.). All rights reserved under International and Pan-American Copyright Conventions. This edition is published by Scholastic Book Services, a division of Scholastic Magazines, Inc., 50 West 44 St., New York, N Y 10036, by arrangement with Random House, Inc.

12 11 10 9 8 7 6 5 4 3 2 1   2   9/7 0 1 2 3 4/8

Printed in the U.S.A.   09

Hey, what are you doing?

Hey!

Look out!

Snoopy, how would you like to play sled dog with me? It's a lot of fun. I'll show you.

Mush! Mush! Let's go!

When I say "Mush,"
you're supposed to pull
the sled.

Argh!!

What in the world is the matter with you? Dogs in the Arctic don't behave like you do.

In the Arctic, dogs are workers. They don't lead prima donna lives.

They have a chain from
their collar that extends
about eight feet. And
unlike you they are tied to
a post or a tree unless they
are going to pull a sled.

This is what you're
supposed to do. You get
into the sled and I'll
show you.

Puff, puff . . . you get
the idea? Puff, puff . . . I
can't take any more,
though. Puff, puff. I
think I'd better go in
and rest up. Puff, puff.

If you were an Arctic dog, you'd be fed only once a day — raw meat, or raw fish, or . . .

You know what's wrong with you? You're overly civilized, Snoopy. That's what's wrong with you!

I hope you can digest all
that food. Good night!

O.K., come on in.

Boy, that must have
been some nightmare!